I0573917

That's What Bears Are For

WRITTEN BY MARILYN HELMER
ILLUSTRATED BY SONIA NADEAU

 PEANUT BUTTER PRESS

*For my arty buddy Sharon and, of course, for Natalia
and Lesya—M.H.*

*To my friends Cathy and Amanda, in loving memory of
"Dee" Sparks and Georgia Morris—S.N.*

Peanut Butter Press
9-1060 Dakota Street
Winnipeg, MB R2N 1P2
www.peanutbutterpress.ca

The artwork in this book was rendered in watercolour.
The text is set in Cheltenham Light.

Book design by Melanie Matheson, Rolling Rhino Communications
Printed and bound in Hong Kong by Paramount Printing Company Limited/Book Art Inc

The hardcover edition of this book is Smyth sewn casebound.
The paperback edition of this book is limp bound.

10 9 8 7 6 5 4 3 2 1

LIBRARY AND ARCHIVES CANADA CATALOGUING IN PUBLICATION

Helmer, Marilyn
        That's what bears are for / written by Marilyn Helmer; illustrated by Sonia Nadeau.

ISBN 978-0-9865329-2-4 (bound). ISBN 978-0-9865329-3-1 (pbk.)

I. Nadeau, Sonia, 1974-   II. Title.

PS8565.E4594T39 2012   jC813'.54   C2012-903598-X

For many years, Bear lived in an attic at the bottom of an old trunk, hoping someday someone would find him. Finally one day, someone did.

The trunk lid flew open. Bear held his breath, remembering long ago days of hugs and cuddles.

A little girl looked down at him. "Momma," she cried. "A bear!" She grabbed Bear and hugged him tightly. Bear's little stitched mouth stretched into a smile.

"He's very old, Jenny," said Momma.
"Older than Grandpa?" Jenny asked.
Momma laughed. "Yes, he's even older than Grandpa. Let's put him on the shelf with your other special toys."

"No, no!" Bear cried. "I'm not a special toy. I'm a bear. Bears are for hugging. Bears are for cuddling."

Jenny must have heard him. All the way downstairs, she hugged Bear and cuddled him. Bear's nose twitched with delight.

In Jenny's room, Momma put Bear high on
a shelf with a doll wearing a silk dress, a china
giraffe, and a Jack-in-the-Box.

"Where did you come from?" asked the doll.

"A trunk in the attic," said Bear.

"I came from Spain," said the doll. "Aren't my clothes beautiful?"

Bear nodded. "Yes, they're very pretty." He didn't have any clothes at all, but he didn't mind a bit.

"You're lucky to be up here with us," said the doll. "Out of harm's way."

"And out of hug's way," Bear said sadly.

The doll shuddered.

"I'm much too delicate for hugging," she said. "You had better sit still. If you fall off the shelf, that little girl will get hold of you."

"But I want to be hugged and cuddled," said Bear. "That's what bears are for."

The doll turned her back on him.

At bedtime that night, Jenny hugged each of
her toys. She blew kisses to the toys on the shelf.
Bear was the only one who smiled back so Jenny
blew him an extra kiss.

Jenny snuggled under the covers and wrapped herself in her soft, fuzzy blanket. Momma kissed her good night and turned out the light. "I love you, Jenny," she said.

"I love you too, Momma," whispered Jenny and
soon she fell fast asleep.

The room was dark and quiet. Bear felt lonely. That's when he had a wonderful idea. He wiggled to the edge of the shelf. "Here I come for hugs and cuddles!" he cried as he tumbled down.

Bear landed on the floor beside Jenny's bed. "Hug me! Cuddle me!" he called out to her. Although Jenny rolled over, she did not wake up.

Bear lay there all night waiting for hugs and cuddles, but Jenny slept on.

The next morning, Momma found Bear on the floor. She put him back on the shelf.

"You're lucky to be up here with us again," said the china giraffe.

"Do ornaments get hugged?" Bear asked.

"Of course not," said the giraffe. "We break too easily."

"I won't break!" said Bear. "I want to be hugged and cuddled. That's what bears are for."

From then on, the giraffe ignored him.

At bedtime, Jenny said good night to her toys and blew kisses to the ones on the shelf. When Bear smiled, she waved her fuzzy blanket at him.

Bear waited until everyone was asleep. He wiggled to the edge of the shelf. "Here I come for hugs and cuddles!" he cried as he somersaulted through the air, landing on the bookcase beside Jenny's bed.

"Hug me! Cuddle me!" he called. Jenny woke up and rubbed her eyes, but she didn't see Bear. "I must have been dreaming," she murmured and went back to sleep.

Bear stayed there all night, waiting for hugs and cuddles, but Jenny slept soundly.

In the morning, Momma put Bear back on the shelf.

The lid of the Jack-in-the-Box flew open and the clown popped up. "It's you again," he said.

Bear nodded. His shoe button eyes were sad.

"Look what happened to me," said the clown. He showed Bear a bend in his spring. "The little girl did that."

"I don't have any springs to bend," said Bear. "I want to be hugged and cuddled. That's what bears are for."

The clown rolled his eyes and disappeared back into his box.

The giraffe and the doll moved farther away from Bear.

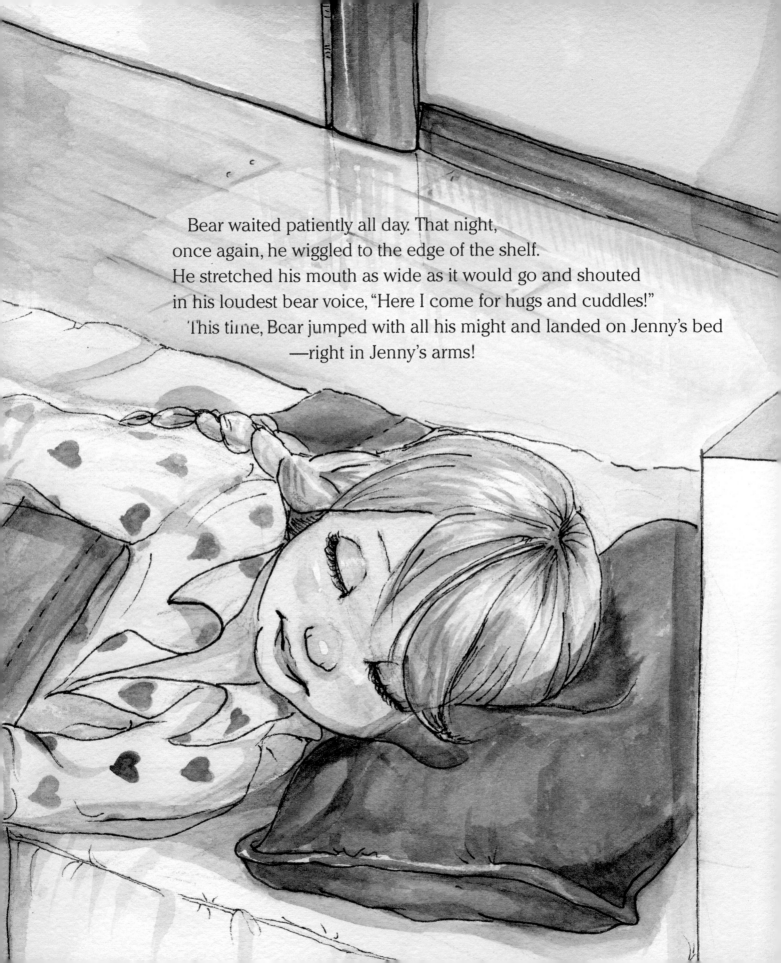

Bear waited patiently all day. That night,
once again, he wiggled to the edge of the shelf.
He stretched his mouth as wide as it would go and shouted
in his loudest bear voice, "Here I come for hugs and cuddles!"
This time, Bear jumped with all his might and landed on Jenny's bed
—right in Jenny's arms!

Jenny opened one eye sleepily. "Oh, Bear,"
she said. "I was dreaming about you."

She hugged Bear and cuddled him until he
thought his little bear heart would burst with joy.

Now every day, Bear and Jenny play together.

When night comes,
Jenny wraps Bear in
her fuzzy blanket.
Then she hugs him
and cuddles him

because all bears,

even very old bears,

even bears as old as Bear is,

love to be hugged and cuddled
more than anything in
the world…

because that's what bears are for!